SHADOWCAST 2

Volume 2: Trapped

Story by
Marv Wolfman

Written by
Scott O. Brown

Illustrated by
Wilson Tortosa

Contents

Steck Vaughn™

A Harcourt Achieve Imprint

www.Steck-Vaughn.com
1-800-531-5015

ALL ABOARD!

Previously...

A dream vacation turns tragic for the families of ten teens who are lost in the middle of the Pacific Ocean.

During an unexpected storm, the ten strangers are forced to find refuge on a chain of desolate islands. As their parents search for any sign that their children are safe, the stranded group begins their search for food and shelter. But during their search, they soon discover they are not alone on the treacherous land. Strange shadows lurk in the ocean mist!

The group has no choice but to work together as they trek across the dangerous island, but they have no idea if they will ever be found.

"I get what I want when I want it!"
—Amira Albertson, 16

"Whatever you say."
— Layla Catava, 15

"Follow me...I know the way."
— Eugene Davis, 15

"I need to work on my jump shot."
— Eduardo Trejo, 17

A severe storm has altered the lives of ten teens who were vacationing with their families on the Tempest, a luxury cruise liner. The storm has forced the ten strangers to seek refuge on an island chain in the middle of the Pacific Ocean.

With no food or shelter, they must work together in order to survive. A dark force, which has haunted these islands for centuries, is watching their every step.

It's so hot! I have to cool off...

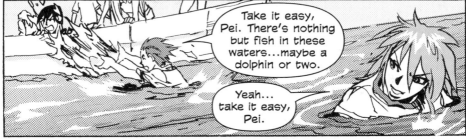

7

Maybe Anne's right. Why don't you get back in the boat, Amira? *AMIRA!*

HELP! AHHH!

I'm just kidding. Calm down.

Hmm.

Well...I'll help you catch the fish, Amira.

All right, but be careful.

Of course.

SPLASH

Everyone is hungry and becoming increasingly weak.

Even Pei starts to realize that eating is more important than finding land.

We'll never catch any fish just using our hands. I have an idea.

Eugene, do you think the next island will be haunted, too?

I don't know, John, but we have to remain calm and work together if we ever want to get back home—

FISH!

HURRY!

The school of fish moves quickly in the water. John and Eugene try to grab as many as they can.

Yes! We got it. Wait...Eugene. You're pulling on the shirt...

...too hard.

It's OK...I've got it!

13

Sure... We can eat the fish...raw.

GROSS!

We'll get sick. We don't even know what kind of fish we're eating.

You've eaten sushi before, haven't you? That's raw fish. What's the difference?

Umm...there's a big difference, but I'm too hungry to care.

We still have to clean the fish, and—

Of course, we'll need to clean the fish first.

I wish Amira would stick a fish in her mouth! I hate being interrupted!

Eugene and Eduardo dive into the water, grabbing sharp ocean rocks that they can use to cut the fish.

These rocks should be sharp enough.

This looks like volcanic rock.

I wonder if the volcanoes on this island are active—

Anne! Take these rocks.

Right... sorry.

This isn't as easy as I thought it would be. I can't cut the fish!

I can't either. I've read about fishing, but I've never actually, well, been fishing.

Layla wants to tell Eduardo to mind his own business, but she decides not to. Everything they've been going through is hard enough, and she doesn't want to start a fight.

The others eat furiously. They've never been this hungry!

Anne has always had a problem trying new things, but she realizes that she must let her hesitations go if she wants to survive this journey.

So... how did it taste?

Well, it wasn't the best thing I've ever had, but it wasn't as bad as I thought it would be. You really need to eat something, Miri. Just try a bite.

Umm... OK.

The food seems to help the group relax. They begin talking to each other. Eduardo and Eugene discuss sports while Cai and Diego talk about art.

Layla and Anne joke with Miri. The more she eats, the more she likes the fish.

You should have seen your face, Miri.

HA!

Most of them make the best of the situation...except Pei, who harbors deep grudges. He thinks everyone should listen to him.

I didn't want to bring this up, but what are we going to do about...tonight?

What do you mean?

I'm not trying to scare anyone, but we all know what we saw on the last island.

Amira, there aren't any ghosts. We saw, I don't know, shadows or something. We were tired and scared.

Come on, Cai. We weren't *that* tired. We have to be realistic.

Realistic? You're talking about ghosts! I'm not sure it's possible to be realistic any longer.

All I'm saying is, we shouldn't just dismiss it. Even if you think we were just seeing shadows, I'm pretty sure they were—

Whatever.

My parents used to tell me the same kind of stories when I was a kid. They were just stories. They weren't true...

...and neither is the cruise director's story. Do you really think that the ghosts of ancient warriors are seeking their lost gold?

Yes.

What? Anne, I think you've read too many books.

Anne is floored by Cai's response.

It's OK, Anne. I'm sure Cai didn't mean what she said.

Oh, come on. Pull yourself together.

Sure I did. Anne is such a baby.

Tempers begin to flare up again as the group prepares to settle in for the night.

The sun sets in the horizon. John checks the compass to see which direction they're traveling.

We're heading west. We should make it to the next island by morning.

John's report is overshadowed by Amira's outburst...

LOOK!

See... I told you.

CHAPTER TWO

The teens try to sleep, but they remain troubled. The unfamiliar sounds prevent the group from resting.

I read this survivor story once, and the people became so hungry that they—

Please, Anne...no more stories.

THUMP

Something hit our boat!

Maybe it was a shark. Oh wait...there aren't any sharks in these waters. Isn't that right, Amira?

THUMP

AHHHH!

Enough! We need to sleep! We're safe in this boat...we can worry about what's out there tomorrow.

Are you two OK?

No... I don't think so.

The sun begins to rise, and everyone slowly wakes up.

Eduardo is the first to notice that they are drifting off course, but that isn't the worst problem.

It's getting really cloudy. I think another storm's coming.

Come on. We have to row faster!

The group panics as they struggle to get to land before the storm hits.

The small boat is very battered. There is no way it can survive another storm.

The teens continue to row against the swelling waves, but as the storm moves in, the wooden boat is tossed against large rocks.

Everyone, hang on!

The waves threaten to toss the teens overboard.

The group defies the torrential rains, as they row faster and faster towards the island. Eduardo and Eugene try to get everyone to safety.

Don't give up. We're going to make it!

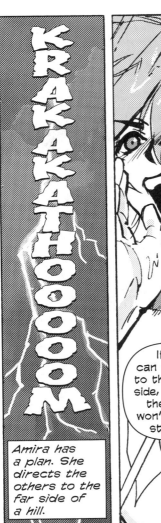

KRAKA THOOOOM

Amira has a plan. She directs the others to the far side of a hill.

If we can make it to the other side, at least the wind won't be as strong.

For once, I agree with her.

It's about a half-mile away. It shouldn't take us very long.

Wait...

...it's raining too hard. I don't think we'll make it.

Do you have a better idea?

Amira is right. We have to keep moving.

If you want to go search for a cave, go ahead, but I'm not going with you.

Fine with me.

Hey, where's Anne and Layla?

Wait here... I'll go back for them.

Soon...

Are you guys OK?

Yeah, we're OK.

I knew Diego wouldn't forget about me...err...us.

Listen to me Amira...this isn't going to work. We're going the wrong way.

No one's listening to me. I'm the one who's right, not Amira. We're not going to survive unless I'm in charge.

John, come here for a second...

Yeah?

Listen...Amira may be right about heading towards the other side of the hill, but she's not thinking straight.

35

John reluctantly agrees with Pei. He's exhausted and doesn't want to stay in the rain any longer.

OK.

Watch out, Anne!

You don't have to push, Miri.

Then walk faster.

Meanwhile, on the Tempest...

...Cai's aunt blames herself for her niece's disappearance.

This is all my fault. If I would've been more strict with Cai, she wouldn't have boarded that boat. She would be safe.

Jean, Anne's mother, tries to comfort her.

It's not your fault. No one predicted the storm... it happened so suddenly.

What? That's why we have a cruise director!

If he would have done his job, our children would be here with us now.

When will the helicopters be here?

They're waiting for the storms to pass. I should hear something soon.

Later...

The storm is passing.

Let's get the others and move out.

Eduardo. Somehow, we have to get the others to listen to us. Pei will be the toughest. He never listens to anyone.

Eduardo and Amira make plans. The other side of the island is several miles away, and they know it will be a dangerous journey.

43

CHAPTER THREE

45

Anne...Diego... I need to talk to you. I need your support. Eduardo and Amira are leading us into danger.

We need to head for the beach and wait there until we're rescued. Our parents will never find us in these trees.

We know the cruise ship is probably sending out a search party. They will find us sooner if we're near the shore.

I don't know what we should do.

So you guys can't sleep, either?

Who can? We're all scared.

Did you say you were scared, Cai?

Uhh...I was uhh...joking. Of course I'm not scared.

Well, I'm scared of everything... spiders, snakes, the dark.

Unable to sleep, the group stays up talking into the night. They're starting to get to know each other a little better.

OK...there *is* something I am scared of, but I'm not telling any of you.

Come on!

Fine! If you must know, I'll tell you.

I'm scared of rats. They creep me out!

Cai...look out! There's a rat!

AHHHH! Where?

HA HA HA

HA HA

HA HA HA HA

Since we can't sleep, maybe we should talk about our next steps. We need to find more food and fresh water.

48

I used to go hunting with my dad. I can help us find food.

I used to go camping a lot with my family. I could help build a shelter if we can find materials, but—

I can help with that, John.

Great! Let's see what we can find.

I don't know how much good I'll be, but I'll try my best.

Meanwhile, on the cruise ship...

What are we going to do?

I'm sure this was all Amira's idea. She's such a troublemaker.

No, you're wrong. The storm separated them from us. It's no one's fault.

Complaining isn't going to help our situation. I want to hear from the captain.

Why haven't we heard from the helicopter pilots?

Mr. Lee has already explained that the weather conditions are causing radio problems.

I know everyone is scared, but I am confident the helicopters will arrive soon.

Their bones ache, but the tired teens continue on their search for food and shelter.

Thanks, Anne. Maybe it wasn't such a bad idea to bring that paddle.

You're welcome, Cai.

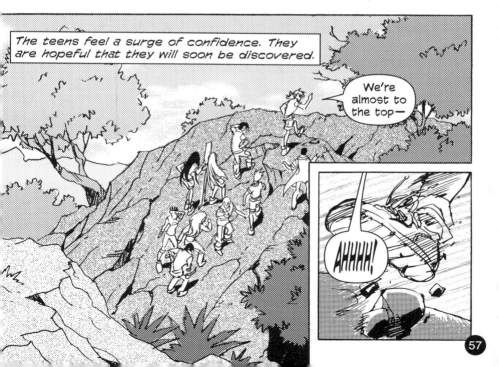

The teens feel a surge of confidence. They are hopeful that they will soon be discovered.

We're almost to the top—

AHHHH!

The others balance Amira as they pass a narrow path on the side of a rocky cliff.

We should've left her behind until we knew we would be safe.

What did you say, Pei?

Uhh... nothing.

We're in this together, Pei.

Sorry, Pei. Layla's right.

Great. The storm is getting worse.

KRAKAK-THOOM

The group seeks shelter from the rain in small dugouts along the hillside.

How are you holding up?

I've been better...but thanks.

Cai, who's usually tough, begins to wonder if they'll actually survive.

What are we going to do?

It's OK, Cai. We're here for each other.

The storm subsides around midnight.

We need to slow down a bit. Amira is hurting pretty badly.

Our parents are never going to find us in this jungle.

I still say we should head towards the beach.

Who's with me?

We're not leaving!

Maybe you're not, but I am.